Oakley
and
Ivan
and the
All-Nighter

To Tatiana, Natalia, and Makai – my reasons why – A.L.

To my husband, Justin, my children, Adrianna,
Christian, and Noah, and to all of my family members
that have participated in this wonderful journey – S.W.

AuthorHouse™
1663 Liberty Drive
Bloomington, IN 47403
www.authorhouse.com
Phone: 833-262-8899

Because of the dynamic nature of the Internet, any web addresses or links contained in this book may have changed
since publication and may no longer be valid. The views expressed in this work are solely those of the author and do
not necessarily reflect the views of the publisher, and the publisher hereby disclaims any responsibility for them.

This book is printed on acid-free paper.

Interior Image Credit: Kaycie Day

ISBN: 978-1-6655-1204-6 (sc)
ISBN: 978-1-6655-1206-0 (hc)
ISBN: 978-1-6655-1205-3 (e)

Library of Congress Control Number: 2020925683

Print information available on the last page.

Published by AuthorHouse 01/26/2021

authorHOUSE®

Oakley and Ivan and the All-Nighter

By: Amanda Lee and Shante Willis

Illustrated by: Kaycie Day

"Good night! Sleep tight! Sleep snug as a bug!"
Said Ivan's mom as she gave him a hug.
"The sun's going down. You need to get rest.
With a big day ahead, you should be at your best."

Tears filled Ivan's eyes 'cause he wanted to play.
He cared not for tomorrow but only today.
Ivan begged to stay up just a little bit more.
His mom firmly said no and walked out his door.

He threw off his covers and jumped out of bed.
Ivan fell to the floor and wishfully said,
"I do not need sleep. My mom is not right.
I want to stay up all day and all night."

Then all of a sudden, an old oak tree shook.
Ivan crept to the window to have a close look.
The night was quite foggy. He hardly could see.
He had a weird feeling about that oak tree.

"Who's there?" he asked in a voice so low.
Then Oakley the Owl softly hooted, "Helloooo!"
Ivan leaped to his bed in total surprise.
The owl could speak and was such a large size!

Ivan gazed into his eyes as Oakley drew near
And an enchanting twinkle began to appear.
At that moment Ivan knew his wish had come true.
He hopped on Oakley's back, and swiftly they flew ...

Through the woods, over clouds, toward the ocean so blue,

Till they came to a beach

and saw a dolphin named Sue.

Sue sang a happy song that filled the air with cheer.
As she greeted Ivan with a splash, he smiled from ear to ear.
Sue jumped and twirled and said, "Come along!
I want you to learn my sweet ocean song.
I know when it's done, great friends we will be."
Then together they sang her sweet melody:

"I love the ocean, and the ocean loves me.
Sand, sun, and seashells as far as I can see.
Ooh, I love the ocean, and the ocean loves me.
Swimming with my friends is as fun as can be."

They dipped and dived through the waves without a care,
Even though the sun was no longer there.
From her nose to her fin she flipped Ivan about.
"We can do this all night!" said Sue with a shout.

"Yippee!" screamed Ivan to all in the sea.
"I'll never need sleep. Sleep's just not for me."
Oakley told Ivan, "There's much more to do."
Ivan jumped on his back, and swiftly they flew ...

Through the valley, over mountains,
toward the trees so green,

Till they came to a rainforest

and saw a toucan named Queen.

Queen moved in a way he had not seen before.
Her wings were spread wide as she swirled
on the floor.
More animals joined in and danced to the beat.
The rhythm made Ivan start tapping his feet.

His tapping turned into a wiggle and bop.
Queen saw him and chuckled 'cause he could not stop.
She asked him to join in her night jamboree,
Where the moon was the only light they could see.

"Come on and have fun. I really do insist.
I'll teach you how to do the tropical twist.
Follow me!" shouted Queen. "Not a step should you miss.
This dance is so easy, and it goes like this:

"Slither to the left. Now shimmy to the right.
Flap your arms like a bird about to take flight.
Stick your tongue out. Spin round and around.
Close your eyes tight, and fall to the ground."

Ivan danced through the night with his rainforest friends,
All while hoping the night would not come to an end.

But as his eyes grew heavy and his dancing slow,
He became a bit sleepy but tried not to show.
When Oakley saw Ivan let out a huge yawn,
He scooped him up, and away they were gone ...

Through the vines, over streams, toward the desert so sandy,

Till they came to a savanna

and saw a giraffe named Mandy.

Mandy stood still, her eyes fixed on the sky.
She was quiet and calm, but Ivan didn't know why.
He moved toward Mandy and tapped on her leg,
But she wouldn't look down so he started to beg.

"Look at me," said Ivan, "I'm ready for more.
My night's been so great. What do you have in store?"
"Your adventure is here in the wonder of night.
The moon is so big. The stars are so bright.
If you look close enough, you can see what I see,"
She whispered to him in a motherly plea.

Ivan sat next to Mandy and heard a loud crash
As large bursts of light filled the sky in a flash—
A million bright stars, each one taking flight
To magically show the tale of his night.

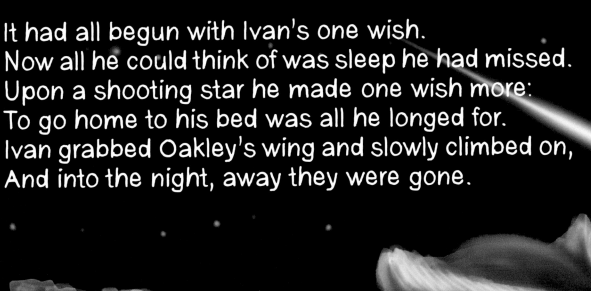

It had all begun with Ivan's one wish.
Now all he could think of was sleep he had missed.
Upon a shooting star he made one wish more:
To go home to his bed was all he longed for.
Ivan grabbed Oakley's wing and slowly climbed on,
And into the night, away they were gone.

Through the wind, over fields, toward
Ivan's house they sped,

Till they came all the way back

to his comfy little bed.

Then Ivan lay down, so ready to rest,
And pulled the covers tight over his chest.
As Oakley began to tiptoe away,
Ivan tugged on his wing and asked him to stay.

"Oh no," said Oakley, "I really must leave.
Tonight I have much more to achieve.
There's one more kid who feels like you,
Whose wish to stay up must also come true.
But count me as your forever friend,
And when you need it, we'll journey again."

As Ivan fell asleep he had a small grin,
For he knew this wasn't really ...

The End.

To learn "Ocean Song" and "Tropical Twist" go to www.OakleyandIvan.com